THE AMAZING SPIDER-MAN

HarperCollins®, ☂®, and HarperFestival® are trademarks of
HarperCollins Publishers.

Evil Comes in Pairs
© 2009 Marvel Entertainment, Inc., and its subsidiaries.
MARVEL, all related characters and the distinctive
likenesses thereof: ™ & © 2009 Marvel Entertainment, Inc.,
and its subsidiaries. Licensed by Marvel Characters B.V.
www.marvel.com. All rights reserved.
Printed in the United States of America.

www.harpercollinschildrens.com
Library of Congress catalog card number: 2008928094
ISBN 978-0-06-162625-8

Book design by John Sazaklis
❖
First Edition

THE AMAZING SPIDER-MAN

VOLUME 1

EVIL COMES IN PAIRS

WRITTEN BY
KATE EGAN

ILLUSTRATED BY
JOE F. MERKEL

HarperFestival®
A Division of HarperCollins Publishers

 # PROLOGUE

PETER PARKER WAS JUST AN ORDINARY HIGH SCHOOL STUDENT—UNTIL HE WAS BITTEN BY A RADIOACTIVE SPIDER AND HIS LIFE CHANGED COMPLETELY. PETER DEVELOPED SUPERHUMAN STRENGTH AND A POWERFUL INNER SENSE THAT PROVIDED HIM WITH EARLY WARNING OF DANGER. LIKE A SPIDER, HE COULD CLING TO MOST SURFACES, CRAWL OVER WALLS, AND SHOOT WEBS.

PETER PARKER HAD BECOME . . .

THE AMAZING SPIDER-MAN

CHAPTER 1

BEEEEP! BEEEEEEEP!! BEEEEEEEEEEP!!!

Peter Parker bolted upright. His alarm clock was ringing loudly enough to wake the next-door neighbors.

"Okay, I can take a hint," Peter muttered in the direction of the ringing.

Peter searched for the clock and eventually found it buried beneath a small mountain of candy wrappers beside his bed. He looked at the time again.

The alarm's been going for half an hour! So much for my resolution to start turning up to work on time, Peter thought. *Oh well, I guess I won't be Employee of the Month any time soon.* Today, he was supposed to work two shifts at the Coffeteria. Peter had been there only a couple of weeks, but he already had a reputation for being late. He threw off his covers and climbed into the first clothes he could find—a crumpled T-shirt and a pair of jeans. Then he ran down the stairs, two at a time, and made a beeline for the kitchen. His aunt May was into all kinds of health food, but she still kept Peter's favorite cereal on hand. He poured himself a heaping bowl and sloshed some milk over the top.

Extra sugary cereal? Good. Soy milk? Bad. Oh, Aunt May!

Peter's things were spread out all over the kitchen table. There were stacks of papers and notebooks—everything he needed to study for his final chemistry exam tomorrow, as well as a copy of yesterday's *Daily Bugle*. In addition to his new job at the coffee shop, Peter was a freelance photographer for the *Bugle*, when he had the time. But right now he didn't have time for *anything*.

Peter noticed his cell phone sitting on top of a pile of books.

"Twelve new messages? I only went to bed three hours ago!" Peter grumbled. "Oh well, what can you do when you're Mr. Popular?"

As he dug into his cereal, Peter dialed the number for his voice mail. The first message was from his friend Harry. *"Take me out to the ball game,"* Harry's voice sang from the phone. "Hey, Peter, I've got tickets to the game tonight. How about you meet me at six and we'll head out together?" The Yankees were playing the Mets, but Peter knew he couldn't go.

"Sorry, Harry, got a big date tonight," Peter said to the cell phone. *A date with the broom at the coffee shop.*

The second message was from one of Peter's chemistry classmates, asking if Peter wanted to study together.

No can do, he thought, rolling his eyes. *I guess I'll just have to get ready for this test in my sleep.*

And the next message was from J. Jonah Jameson, the publisher of the *Daily Bugle.* "Parker! Long time, no hear!" he barked. "Where've you been? If I don't see your sorry face around here sometime soon, you'll be out of a job. How do you expect me to sell any papers without pictures of that webbed menace?"

Well, since you asked so nicely, Peter thought. He

snapped his phone shut, frustrated. Jameson wanted him to take photos of Spider-Man for the newspaper. One small problem: He *was* Spider-Man. And right now Peter was busy with a million other things. He didn't have time to set up a photo shoot starring himself! He put his face in his hands and rubbed his forehead.

As Spider-Man, Peter Parker stopped crime all over New York City, and he knew that was important. But school and friends, making money to help Aunt May pay the bills—they were all important, too. And nobody, not even a Super Hero, could do it all at once.

CHAPTER 2

IT TOOK PETER AN HOUR on the subway to get to the Coffeteria from the quiet neighborhood where he lived with his aunt May. Peter was so tired from all the late nights, he forgot his frustration and fell asleep. By the time his stop finally came, he almost missed it.

"Wait!" Peter called out to no one in particular. "I need to get off!"

A large man yelled, "Hey, kid! Some of us want to get to work on time. You can't hold the train doors!"

"Sheesh! Good morning to you, too," Peter shot back weakly as the two metal doors reopened long enough for him to make his escape onto the platform.

He climbed the stairs into the crowded streets of midtown Manhattan. Tourists thronged the sidewalks.

If it was possible, the city was going to be even busier than usual. Today was the city's annual Celebrate New York parade.

If I'm lucky, maybe I'll catch a glimpse from a window in the coffee shop, Peter thought, as he trudged toward the café.

He passed a blue van pulled up at the curb. The engine was running, but there was no driver.

I'm no genius, but I've got a feeling this isn't your friendly church carpool, Peter thought. *Who would be crazy enough to leave a van unattended anywhere near Midtown on parade day?*

Peter looked at his watch and frowned: 9:58. He was due at the coffee shop in two minutes. He didn't want to be late for work *again*, but somebody had to check out that van.

I don't see any other Super Heroes around, so I guess that somebody is me.

When he got to the van, Peter stopped and bent down to tie the lace of his sneaker. *Very smooth,* he thought. *I'm just a guy tying his shoes. No need to pay attention to me. Carry on with your suspicious—and most likely criminal—activity.*

From the corner of his eye, Peter could see three men behind the van. They were all dressed in black clothing. And they were wearing ski masks!

Black clothes. Masks. Again, I'm no genius, thought Peter, *but this is definitely not a church carpool.*

The coffee shop would just have to wait.

CHAPTER 3

PETER DUCKED INTO A NEARBY side street and changed into his spider-suit. In a red and blue flash, he did a somersault and flipped himself onto the wall of the closest building, sticking there by his hands and feet.

Surveying the scene, Spider-Man saw the men heading in the direction of a fancy shop on the opposite side of the street.

As the shopkeeper opened the door of the store, one of the men pushed the older man out of the way, and all three stormed inside.

Spidey swung up the wall above the store's main entrance and lowered himself slowly along the side of the brick building. *Things are about to get very sticky,* he thought.

Once he was inside, Spidey could hear the leader of the group yelling at an employee, "Get out of the way! Do what we say and maybe nobody will get hurt!"

"Yeah, nobody but you!" Spidey shot back, just as the crook had filled his arms with several handbags.

Spidey fired a flurry of web-lines at the thief. Covered in sticky stuff from head to toe, he cried out, "Aaargh!"

"Ding! Ding! You're the winner!" Spidey called. "Grand prize for being customer number one this morning!"

In the meantime, another robber had smashed a glass display case and was quickly filling his sack with fistfuls of glittering jewels. Spidey shot a silk strand in the criminal's direction and easily wrapped him in a tight web cocoon.

The third thief stood by the cash register behind Spidey, ready to attack. Even though Spider-Man could not see behind him, his spider-sense tingled.

"Fancy seeing you here!" Spidey called out, as he spun around to wrap the last of the trio in a thick layer of webbing.

Soon, all three bandits were tied up.

Things are about to get very sticky.

Would-be customers had gathered on the sidewalk to watch. The robbery in progress didn't seem to bother them. If anything, it seemed to make them more excited about being in New York!

"Get my camera, honey!" a woman called out. "That's Spider-Man!" A heavy man with sweat covering his brow pulled out a camera from his fanny pack and handed it over to the woman.

Click. Click. Click.

The sudden flashes made Spider-Man dizzy for a brief second. "All right, all right, people," he muttered once he had recovered. "Nothing more to see here. Isn't there a big building somewhere else in the city you want to take pictures of to show the folks back home?"

The store manager rushed to the scene and began to clear the webbing with a broom. "What a mess!" he complained. "I'm trying to run a business here."

Spider-Man shook his head. Typical New York lack of gratitude! "You're welcome, sir," he called, and webbed away.

CHAPTER 4

"WHERE HAVE YOU BEEN, PARKER?" his manager, Sally, hissed at him as he entered the coffee shop. "You're almost an hour late, and in case you haven't noticed, we're really busy!"

Peter started to explain, "Sorry, I was—"

"Never mind. Go clean yourself up and get out here!" Sally made an angry gesture at the small bit of web goo stuck to Peter's shirt.

Great, Peter thought, *now she thinks I'm unreliable* and *dirty.*

Outside the coffee shop, the streets were beginning to fill with people gathering for the parade. Soon the police would arrive to make sure nobody caused any trouble.

Or that was the plan, anyway. But it wasn't the only plan afoot.

❊ ❊ ❊

In a nearby subway tunnel, somebody was lurking, gathering strength. For now, he had to stay in the shadows, hide where nobody could see him or guess what he had in store for New York. Carnage was his name, and Carnage was his game.

The light from an oncoming train shone on Carnage for a moment. He was an enormous beast. He had muscled arms and legs that looked inhuman, foot-long claws, and teeth as sharp as daggers. His fiery red color made him even more frightening.

In spite of his size, Carnage moved with surprising ease. In a split second, he squeezed against the tunnel's wall as the train screeched sharply around a corner and coasted to a stop at the station. Carnage was ready!

There was only one problem: Spider-Man was in the neighborhood today. Carnage had seen Spider-Man's run-in with the masked thieves earlier that morning. Carnage was not one of Spider-Man's biggest fans. In fact, he was very, very angry with him. Spider-Man had ruined his plans before.

Carnage was ready!

But this time, Carnage thought, *things will be different.* Carnage had backup: his old jailhouse buddy, Venom.

Venom hated Spider-Man for his own reasons, and Carnage knew he would be able to convince Venom to join forces with him against Spidey. Carnage just needed to find Venom.

Last Carnage had heard, Venom was across the river in New Jersey.

Moving with superhuman speed, Carnage made his way through the subway tunnels all the way to Times Square. There he discovered that the tunnel he was in did not connect to New Jersey. Roaring with frustration, Carnage leaped up onto the subway platform. Frightened commuters scattered in all directions, frantically seeking escape.

Carnage fired a web-line toward the top of a staircase and swung himself upward. Once in the daylight, he hurried across the city, weaving around the gridlock of cars and running into the Lincoln Tunnel. Under the cover of darkness, he scaled the side of a delivery van and flattened himself beneath the tunnel's roof. Carnage crept across the tops of the stopped cars, pausing every now and then to leave a vicious dent in the most expensive models.

"I hope you're ready to come out and play, Venom," Carnage hissed. "Because I'm on my way!"

CHAPTER 5

PETER WAITED UNTIL SALLY'S BACK was turned before making himself a double espresso.

The breakfast rush had just ended, with only a few people scattered around reading the morning papers. From across the room, Peter caught a glimpse of the *Daily Bugle*. CAT BURGLAR PUTS A JINX ON NEW YORK, Peter read the front-page headline.

Who is this new cat on the scene? Peter wondered. But there was no time to think about that now. People were already streaming through the door again.

"It's parade day," Sally said from behind him. "It's going to be busy all day." As if Peter had somehow forgotten.

Peter stood behind the glass counter while a young couple looked at the pastries on display. "Should I get the apple coffee cake?" the woman asked her husband. "Although that chocolate doughnut looks delicious . . . No, let's make it a raspberry muffin with a double cappuccino." Then the man ordered a bagel with cream cheese on the side. The person after him ordered a roll with butter, and his two kids needed high chairs and sippy cups. . . .

Head is spinning, Peter thought. "Anyone want just plain old coffee?" he asked hopefully. The father of the toddlers gave him an irritated look.

Somehow Peter managed to keep the orders straight until—

"Hey, you!" A woman with graying hair was gesturing impatiently at Peter with her cup of coffee. "Could I get soy milk over here?"

"Half and half!" someone else called out from the opposite direction.

When Peter mixed the two orders up by mistake, the old woman was unforgiving.

"Does this smell like soy milk to you? I asked for soy milk!" The lady was speaking more loudly with each breath.

"I-I'm sorry," Peter stammered.

"Is there a manager I can speak to?"

And just as Peter had managed to sweet-talk the customer out of having her heart-to-heart with Sally, he noticed the first couple who had ordered walking out the door.

"Hey, you haven't paid your—" Peter started to shout, but the door had already closed behind the couple.

If I don't get free food around here, they don't either, Peter thought. Decision time. He was pretty sure Sally wouldn't want him leaving. On the other hand, she wouldn't want people stiffing her. . . .

All right, I'm going to make a run for it. Those two need a talking-to.

The sidewalk was crowded with pedestrians and street vendors. Peter didn't need his spider-sense to track the couple, though. They were halfway down the block, looking at a map.

Panting, Peter ran up to them. "Forget something?" he asked, waving the bill in front of them.

"Is there a problem?" the man replied calmly.

"Just that people usually pay for breakfast at our place," Peter snapped.

The man retorted, "You never even brought us our bill. I assumed that meant breakfast was on the house." He smirked at Peter.

"You eat, you pay. Pretty simple idea!"

Finally, the man reached for his wallet and pulled out a ten-dollar bill, four cents more than what he owed. "Keep the change," he said, and turned away.

"Thanks, big spender," Peter called after him.

The nerve! he thought, stifling the urge to chase the man down and fling him into the air. Peter had what he needed, and that was enough. It was his good deed for the day.

Not that Sally saw it in quite the same way. "I can't believe I have to tell you this," she said, shaking her head when she saw him return. "You are not to leave the premises when you're working."

"But those people—"

Sally held up her hand and closed her eyes for a second.

"Not on my time," she said. "There are orders to take."

Some days Peter Parker just couldn't win.

CHAPTER 6

CARNAGE FLUNG HIS ARMS WIDE open. From each pointed claw, red and silver spears formed and detached themselves. The spears flew high into the air before landing on the hood of a rusted car. "Looks like I've still got the touch. With my moves and Venom on my side, that spider is going down!" Carnage cried out to the vacant lot.

Carnage picked his way across the lot, stepping around heaps of trash and hoping for some sign that Venom was near. *Come on, Venom,* Carnage thought, *where are you? We have a city to destroy.*

A plane roared above him, preparing to land at a nearby airport. Watching its wheels come down, Carnage spotted a warehouse that he hadn't noticed before and felt immediately drawn to it. He hissed with satisfaction. Venom was in there. Carnage could feel him.

One of the reasons Carnage had chosen Venom as his partner in crime was Venom's hatred for Spider-Man. The other reason was that Venom and Carnage shared a very unusual bond. Both of them had been taken over by the same alien being. The alien gave them their superpowers. It also gave them a connection that couldn't be broken. If Venom was anywhere nearby, Carnage could sense him. This awareness worked both ways, too.

The alien had also tried to take over Spider-Man. But Spider-Man had resisted. He had rejected the alien's powers. Carnage scowled at the thought. Just another reason to hate the wall-crawler. "Spineless weakling!" he growled.

The warehouse windows were shattered, its roof half caved in. Carnage stepped carefully into the stairwell, knowing that his giant bulk could send the floors crashing down at any minute.

"Getting closer, my friend," Carnage cackled. He shot a web-line to the top of the stairs and swung himself upward until he was at the landing. "Reunion time!"

When he stepped inside the big empty room, Carnage was overcome by the stench of mold and rot.

"Oh, Venom, you really need to shower," Carnage called out, as he scanned the room. He ran the sharp, red tips of his talons across the floorboard, clearing a layer of dust. "And you need a maid—this place is filthy."

Suddenly, two thick web-lines flew at Carnage, wrapping around his ankles. He felt a strong tug. In a red blur, he was webbed to a beam in the ceiling, where he hung upside down!

"*Venom!*" he roared.

Carnage saw Venom move out of the shadows. "What do you want? Why are you here?" Venom growled.

Carnage controlled his urge to lash back at Venom, to break free of the web as he knew he could do so easily. Venom's suspicion was only natural. He would have to play nice if he wanted Venom on his team.

"I'm here to help you," Carnage said carefully.

Venom cackled. "So now you're one of the good guys? That's not what I've heard."

"And that's not what I mean," Carnage retorted. "I'm here to help you with something you've wanted for a long time."

"Which is . . . what?" Venom asked suspiciously.

"Let me down and I'll tell you."

Venom paused for a moment before shooting another web-line at the ceiling beam. The line cracked like a whip, shattering the beam.

CRASH!

As Carnage hurtled to the floor, he yelled, *"Aargh!"*

The broken pieces that used to be the beam flew in every direction, leaving behind clouds of gray dust. After cutting himself loose from the remains of Venom's webbing, Carnage spoke.

"We're old friends—no need to beat around the bush. I want to stop that spider once and for all."

At the mention of Spider-Man, Venom tensed. His face

was covered in a black mask, but Carnage could tell from the glint in his eyes that Venom still hated Spider-Man.

"Why now?" Venom barked impatiently. As he spoke, he paced back and forth. His muscular body covered in the black suit was a severe contrast to Carnage's blazing red. "And why do you need *me*?"

"Why now?" roared Carnage. "Because I'm tired of seeing Spider-Man's face plastered on the front of every newspaper! Because I'm sick of hearing him being hailed as a hero. Because he should have been destroyed a long time ago!"

"Why should I help you?" Venom asked. His biceps rippled.

"Oh, it's just me, huh?" Carnage mocked, stepping closer to Venom. "You don't hate Spider-Man for putting you out of a job as Eddie Brock at the *New York Globe*? Little Eddie thought he had a big story. He found the scary serial killer. He was supposed to be the big shot at the newspaper who reported the story."

"Watch it, Carnage!" Venom thundered.

"Until Spider-Man came along and caught the *real* serial killer. Poor you! No longer a hero."

Furious, Venom jumped into the air and slammed into Carnage's chest, feetfirst. "I'm warning you!" Venom shouted so loudly, the walls of the old warehouse shook.

Laughing, Carnage got up. He shook debris off his suit. "So many reasons for you to join me, Venom. What do you say?"

A heavy silence filled the moldy room. Finally Venom smiled, exposing razor-sharp, jagged teeth.

"Count me in!"

Carnage held out his massive hand for Venom to shake. For a moment he thought about telling Venom the rest of his plan, but he decided that wasn't necessary. Venom could be squeamish sometimes. What Carnage was planning was much bigger than Spider-Man, but what Venom didn't know wouldn't hurt him.

"Welcome," Carnage said, as his lips curled into a smile.

CHAPTER

PETER SAT IN THE BREAK room at the back of the Coffeteria, his aching feet resting on a chair. *What can I do that doesn't involve moving my arms or my legs?* he wondered.

Outside the coffee shop, the sky was just beginning to darken. The parade would start soon.

Meanwhile, the newly formed duo of Carnage and Venom fired web-lines toward a metal grate above the train platform at Times Square and pulled themselves up. First Carnage and then Venom burst through the metal and into the streets, where they were greeted by a growing crowd.

"Awesome special effects!" a young guy exclaimed. "This parade gets better and better every year."

The throngs of people seemed convinced that

Carnage and Venom were parade performers, but the two of them weren't taking any chances. They disappeared into a dark alley right away.

"Where is Spider-Man?" Venom snarled. He was ready to go!

"You tell me," said Carnage. "You're the one who can sense him."

Closing his eyes, Venom concentrated for a moment. Then his eyes snapped open.

"That way," he said, pointing east.

Carnage bared his teeth in glee. "Lead on!"

Swinging across town on his webbing, Carnage hung low enough on the downturns to knock out a few pedestrians along the way. Then suddenly, he was slammed against a wall with Venom's glare fixed on him.

"What do you think you're doing?" Venom sneered. "Advertising to everyone that you're here? Next thing you know, the cops will be on our tail."

Cops. As if they mattered. Besides, Carnage *wanted* the cops to come after him. That was part of his plan.

"Yeah? And?" he prompted Venom.

Venom's eyes narrowed. "They're a distraction we don't need. What if they warn Spider-Man?"

Carnage scowled, but decided to behave. He needed to keep Venom happy.

Venom and Carnage scuttled up and down the sides of office buildings, their feet sticking to glass walls. They scaled towers and swung over avenues.

Finally, Venom dropped down to street level. Carnage could see a shoe store, a newsstand, and a coffee shop on the block.

Venom's eyes glowed bright as he looked at the yellow and blue sign of the Coffeteria. "This is it," he said to Carnage. "I can feel him. The crawler is in there."

CHAPTER 8

PETER WAS IN THE BREAK room, checking his voice mail on his cell phone, when he heard a commotion out in the restaurant. Peering around the corner, he saw a pack of people all turned away from him. They seemed terrified by something he couldn't quite see.

Another attempted robbery? Peter wondered. *You have got to be kidding me!*

And why wasn't his spider-sense tingling? That was weird.

Peter peeked into the front of the shop. Carnage! Venom! What were his two archenemies doing here? Together?!

Looking for blood, he thought. *My blood.*

At least that explained the lack of warning from his

spider-sense. Carnage and Venom could make it blank out when they were nearby.

"Just what I need today," Peter said under his breath.

Carnage had pulled the customers together in a tight knot of webbing. Now, as they watched, he was laying waste to the place. He slashed open bags of coffee, tipped over tanks of boiling water, broke tables, and threw chairs out the plateglass window.

At least I've got the home-court advantage. This game ain't over, Peter thought.

Peter slipped into the bathroom for a quick change and stormed out as Spider-Man.

"Can I take your order?" he asked Venom.

Venom lunged for Spider-Man, but before he could make contact, Spider-Man fired a web toward the light fixture on the ceiling. Using his spider-strength, he pulled himself upward and hung from the light. He pointed toward the terrified people below.

"Helpless tourists in Bermuda shorts?" Spider-Man

asked mockingly. "Carnage, Venom, have you really sunk this low?"

"Keep talking, spider!" Carnage spat. "It's over for you now—it's two against one!"

Meanwhile, Venom yanked the web away from the bound customers and chased them out the door. Then he turned to face Spider-Man, a vein throbbing in his thick neck. "You're right," he hissed. "No point in hurting them. You're the one we're after, webhead!"

"Really?" Spider-Man shot back. "Thought you guys were just grabbing a skim latte after some sightseeing. Don't I feel special!"

Spider-Man jumped down from the light and stepped over the broken mugs and mountains of ground coffee on the floor. "Last one to the kitchen is . . . a scary, evil villain with bad teeth!" Spidey called.

As soon as he entered the kitchen, Spidey launched several webs to open the knife drawers and then yanked their contents toward himself.

He was pretty sure he could hold off these guys with

"It's over for you now—it's two against one!"

whatever he had on hand. But then Carnage got close, right up in his face. Carnage's skin rippled for a second. A piece of it broke off and formed into a shining cleaver sharper than any Spider-Man had ever seen.

Whoa, Spider-Man thought. *I forgot he could do that. I guess these butter knives won't cut it after all.*

There was an industrial-size coffee grinder in the corner behind Carnage. Spider-Man fired a web-line at the grinder's power switch. As the blades whirred into action, he yanked the machine toward Carnage. "Want some coffee, Carnage?" Spidey asked.

Like lightning, Carnage flung the blade from his claws. The cleaver flew in midair and landed on the grinder's power cord, slicing it in half.

POP! POP! Pop! Pop.

Carnage laughed. "Rest in peace, Mr. Coffee. You're next, spider!" Retreating a few steps, he continued his taunt. "Venom, you want to take a shot at the spider? It's fun!"

In a flash, Venom shot out a long web that wrapped around Spider-Man. Venom tossed him toward the ceiling—

and the rapidly rotating fan that was fixed there!

Whap! Whap!

The metal fan blades slashed at Spider-Man's suit, and his skin. *"Aahhhh!"* Spidey yelled.

Spider-Man struggled to get loose. But his body was tightly bound in place by layers of Venom's webbing. The fan spun around and around, pummeling him. Gathering every ounce of his strength, Spider-Man finally jerked himself free from the blades and fell hard to the floor.

Carnage came at Spidey with a long fork, and Venom opened an oven that had been on for hours.

Spider-Man's mind raced. *I'm about to be roasted by two very rude customers,* he thought. *Got to think fast.*

Then suddenly, sirens were wailing outside. Spider-Man braced himself for what would come next—the cops didn't stand a chance. But Carnage shocked him by soaring through the grimy back window and taking off at top speed!

"Your time will come, Spider-Man," Carnage called back. "Lucky for you it's not now!"

Spider-Man thought he detected a confused look on Venom's face before Venom followed Carnage through the window. And then the bad guys were gone, as quickly as they had come.

VENOM AND CARNAGE HAD VANISHED, but Spider-Man was determined to find them. Nobody was safe as long as those two were on the streets.

Still bound by Venom's webbing, Spidey rolled around on the floor for several minutes. Eventually, he recovered his strength and was able to break the webbing apart, freeing himself.

Well, that was bizarre, Spider-Man thought. *And painful.* Why had Carnage and Venom taken off when the police arrived? Each of them alone could crush the police and together they were even stronger. *Since when are they the types to shy away from a good brawl?* Something didn't add up.

Spider-Man slipped out the back entrance of the coffee shop and made his way around to the front. A crowd of people were gathered there. He could hear Sally wailing about the damage to the shop. "What a mess! We're going to have to shut down for days to repair all this," she groaned. Then her tone grew angry. "Where's Parker? How does that guy manage to disappear every time there's work to be done? I've got some news for him: He's fired."

Under his mask, Spider-Man gritted his teeth. *I just can't catch a break, can I?* he thought. Being a Super Hero was really hard sometimes.

But there was no time to brood about it now. Spider-Man had bad guys to catch and a city to save. Even though he was pretty sure no one would bother to thank him for it.

Spider-Man's spider-sense told him which direction Venom and Carnage were moving: North. The fact that he could sense them meant that they weren't very close by. They had a head start.

Spider-Man set off northward, clinging to buildings

and avoiding the crowds. He prowled along the edge of Central Park to the Metropolitan Museum of Art, where the parade was set to kick off. A grandstand stood across the street, covered in bright fabric and surrounded by rows of bleachers for important people who hadn't arrived yet. Groups of marchers were forming, and clusters of musicians were getting in their final practices. Spider-Man couldn't see Venom or Carnage, and his spider-sense wasn't giving him any clues either. His instincts, though, told him that he had better not get too comfortable.

Then Spider-Man spotted a Mobile Police Unit trailer. Perfect. Unlike his enemies, he was on good terms with the authorities.

Spidey knocked on the door, but nobody answered. Impatiently, he webbed the door and ripped out the lock. He stepped inside and pulled it shut behind him.

What is all this? Spider-Man wondered. There were no friendly police officers eating doughnuts and drinking coffee. Instead, he saw stacks and stacks of deadly weapons. *These definitely aren't police property. The police don't get toys this deadly. So who put this stuff here?*

He had a pretty good idea.

This was why Carnage and Venom didn't want to face the cops at the coffee shop, he guessed. *They didn't want to get distracted before they could carry out their bigger plan.*

Spider-Man didn't know quite what the plan was, but one thing was beyond doubt: There were enough weapons here to do some *serious* damage.

AFTER SEALING OFF THE ENTIRE trailer with webbing, Spider-Man continued on his search for Carnage and Venom. Led by his spider-sense, he kept moving—until his senses deadened, suddenly and completely.

Why did my spider-sense stop tingling? Peter thought. Then he realized the reason.

Spider-Man couldn't feel the presence of Carnage and Venom at all. That meant they were either both out of range and up to more mischief—or right up close and throwing off his spider-sense.

Well, they wouldn't go too far away from their little toy box of weapons . . . but I don't see them anywhere.

Spider-Man webbed to the roof of the Metropolitan Museum and clung there, hoping his spider-sense would kick in.

But he felt no tingling. Just a pinching feeling in his midsection. "Whoa," Spidey murmured, as his stomach rumbled loudly. "That's a little embarrassing."

With that, he realized he was *starving*. He hadn't eaten anything since that bowl of cereal at Aunt May's, hours ago. *Even Super Heroes have to eat,* thought Spider-Man. And there was a hot-dog vendor, conveniently located right there on the steps of the museum.

He jumped down to the stone steps. "Hi, could I get a hot dog with mustard and onions on it?" Spidey asked.

"Care for a side order with that?" the vendor asked. His voice took on a taunting tone. "How about a *punch*?"

Huh? Spider-Man wondered. Then the vendor's face seemed to ripple. Within seconds, he had morphed into Venom, his head busting through the umbrella of the hot-dog stand. Shaking it free, he tore after Spider-Man with his fists flying.

Of course! Spider-Man thought. *Venom has the ability to morph into different shapes!*

Spider-Man shot a long strand to the column at the museum's entrance and webbed himself to the roof. Instantly, he shot out another web and swung to the roof of an apartment building across the street. Spidey stepped on Venom's strand, breaking it in half to stop him from following.

To defeat the combined powers of Venom and Carnage, Spider-Man would have to be more than just strong. He would have to be clever.

The roof he had landed on boasted a couple of palm trees and a full-size swimming pool—it was a five-star hotel. With a quick glance around, Spider-Man decided to ambush the evil duo from behind the poolside bar.

When Spider-Man crouched back there, though, he found the spot was already taken. By Carnage.

"Look, Venom, I found an itsy-bitsy spider!" Carnage called.

Carnage fired two sharp knives from his claws. Spider-

Man dodged, and the knives missed him, but just barely. He was still regaining his balance when Carnage tackled him to the ground, holding him by the wrists.

Spider-Man shot out a clump of webbing, making it hard for Carnage to grip him. As Carnage snapped and snarled with rage, Spider-Man twisted free.

"Looks like spiders aren't so easy to catch," Spider-Man taunted.

From another corner of the roof, Venom hurled three pool chairs at Spider-Man. Two of them bounced off Spidey's head. The third landed on his outstretched arm.

THOOM!

Venom and Carnage each folded their powerful arms around their knees and slammed into Spider-Man's chest. All three landed in the pool, and then Venom and Carnage tried to keep Spider-Man down!

"What's wrong? Spiders can't swim?" Venom laughed, as Spider-Man thrashed.

"Once we finish him off," Carnage crowed to Venom, "we're going straight to the parade!"

"What's wrong? Spiders can't swim?"

"Parade?" Venom replied. "What's at the parade?"

"I'll tell you later," Carnage promised. "First things first." His biceps bulged as he shoved Spider-Man's head under the surface of the pool.

Spider-Man fought down an instant of panic as Carnage and Venom held him underwater. *This is all good,* he told himself. He could hold his breath for a long time, and the villains' greater weight wasn't much of an advantage underwater.

Play it right, he thought. *Let them think they've won. . . .*

Spider-Man tried to calm his heart rate. *I knew they had a bigger plan,* he thought. So his earlier guess about the Mobile Police Unit had been right. But who was the target? And why were there so many weapons?

I have to stop them!

With what was left of his strength, Spider-Man burst out from under the water, sputtering. Then he shot out two thick webs, wrapping one each around the villains' heads and pounding them together.

"Hey, gents," Spider-Man gasped, "I don't know this pool game. Maybe we could just play Marco Polo instead."

CHAPTER 11

IN THE MOMENT THE VILLAINS needed to recover, Spider-Man ducked inside the hotel and took the elevator to the ground floor, soaking wet.

If what I remember about Venom still holds true, the hotel is the safest place, Spider-Man reasoned. *Venom is a softie when it comes to hurting civilians, and this place is packed with them.*

In the lobby, Spidey scored a towel for drying himself off and a box of Band-Aids for his cuts. He made a face as he checked out the dozens of new ones Carnage had made with the broken glass. "I'm starting to feel like a pincushion," he muttered.

Outside, the parade was poised to begin. A marching band stood in formation, rehearsing a final time and waiting for the go-ahead from the grand marshal. The music was deafening.

Looking up, Spider-Man saw Carnage and Venom fly off the roof and into the center of the band, just as it received its marching orders. With Venom and Carnage still in their midst, the band launched into the song "New York, New York" and headed downtown. Spider-Man watched in puzzlement as Carnage clapped his hands to his ears.

Suddenly, Spidey remembered something. *The last time we played together, Carnage went berserk when he chased me into a rock concert. He hates loud noises, so this music must be killing him. Idea alert!*

From what he had overheard, Spider-Man suspected Carnage had not filled Venom in on all his plans. That could be a useful thing. . . .

Spider-Man sped out of the hotel. He shot a web toward a window ledge on the building across the street, pulled upward, and stuck close to the wall, hanging on by his hands and feet. Then he swung to the sidewalk a block ahead of Venom and Carnage.

The villains saw Spider-Man immediately. Using himself as bait, Spider-Man led them right to the playground he'd noted earlier. The Mobile Police Unit still stood in its corner, undisturbed.

The playground was crowded with children, swinging and sliding and screaming. One girl asked Spider-Man for his autograph, while Venom and Carnage stood behind a parked car, glowering. They weren't exactly good with kids.

Spider-Man had timed it just right. He knew Venom would be able to keep Carnage from rampaging through the playground for a few minutes. And a few minutes was all he needed. When the parade began streaming past, the kids ran in every direction to see it. Soon they were out of the playground, dancing to the music and begging their parents for cotton candy.

Kids out of harm's way—check, Spidey thought.

Venom and Carnage were edging toward Spider-Man again, ready to attack now that their audience had disappeared. "Hey, gentlemen, what's this all about?" Spider-Man asked mockingly, gesturing toward the trailer full of weapons. "You've got a lot of fancy stuff in there. Planning a tea party?"

Venom looked at Carnage blankly, "What's the spider talking about?"

Carnage was creeping toward the trailer, trying to protect his weapons.

Spider-Man pressed on, now sure that he had guessed right. Whatever Carnage was planning, Venom wasn't part of it. "So, seriously now, who else is going down today?" Spidey threw out. "Lots of kids around. Are they on the agenda?"

He stole a glance at Venom's face and could tell Venom didn't like the sound of this at all. If there was one thing Venom hated more than Spider-Man, it was hurting innocent people.

"Wait a minute," Venom started, "I thought we were just going to take care of our spider problem—"

Carnage snarled. "We *will* take care of the spider! As for the rest—don't be such a baby, Venom!"

"No!" Venom snapped, and began backing away. "I didn't sign up for all this."

"Too late!" Carnage lunged at Venom. "You're in."

"Wrong!" Venom called out. He somersaulted over Carnage's head and landed on his feet outside the playground. "You're on your own, Carnage!"

And he took off through the park.

CHAPTER

AS CARNAGE GLARED AFTER VENOM, Spider-Man shot past him and hurtled over the playground fence. "Looks like it's just me and you. Cozy!" he called.

He webbed a passing parade float and swung into the grandstand, where dignitaries had now gathered to watch the parade. He spotted the mayor, some movie stars, some sports figures, and . . . yes, there he was—the chief of police.

Spider-Man crept through the crowd until he reached the police chief and then whispered in his ear, "Trouble in the playground." In case the chief didn't know what he was talking about, Spidey jabbed a thumb in the direction he'd come from. He had a plan for Carnage, but it wouldn't do to leave all those weapons unattended, even if the trailer was bound by his webbing from earlier.

Carnage was still on his tail, but where Spidey took care not to crush the spectators, Carnage wasn't so thoughtful. Sirens screamed in the distance as police reinforcements headed toward the scene.

"Can't take me on your own?" Carnage said to Spider-Man, sneering. "Need a little backup?"

"Nope," Spider-Man snapped. "Just wanted to share the fun with some friends."

He moved toward the center of the grandstand, where a podium had been set up for the mayor to give a speech. A microphone and speakers were there for him, along with a glass of water and a copy of his speech. Spider-Man waited until Carnage was practically next to him, aching for some hand-to-hand combat. Then, working quickly, he webbed Carnage to the speakers.

Carnage laughed. "You think you're a smart little spider, don't you? But that trailer is only one of many! After I'm

"You think you're a smart little spider, don't you?"

through here, there will be no nice police officers enforcing the laws. No mayor making sure there's order. A weapon in the hands of every man and woman. A city without laws. A city without limits!"

"Where do you get these nutty ideas?" Spider-Man responded. "I think you've been hanging out with the wrong crowd!"

Before Carnage could retaliate, Spider-Man pressed the microphone to the speakers, right next to Carnage's ear!

The blast of feedback was painful to Spider-Man. But to Carnage, it was almost deadly. Spider-Man watched as his enemy stiffened, his eyes bulging. Then Carnage went limp. He sagged in the sticky web, his head rolling from side to side.

Carnage was still down for the count when the police hauled him off in their sturdiest wagon.

Spider-Man ducked into a nearby portable toilet and changed into his regular clothes. Time to go home.

Settling back in his seat on the subway, Peter Parker closed his eyes. *Some day,* he thought. *On the plus side, I* saved New York City, and I put a crazy villain back behind bars. On the minus side, I lost my job. And I've got an exam tomorrow!

He checked his watch and saw it was still early evening. There was still time to hit the books. Or . . .

Maybe I'll call Harry and check out that game after all.

"Chemistry can wait. I think I've earned the night off!" Peter said aloud.

IN HIS NEXT ADVENTURE, SPIDEY'S IN FOR SOME BAD LUCK WHEN HE CROSSES PATHS WITH THE BLACK CAT!

ILLUSTRATION BY JOHN SAZAKLIS